Which Witch Is Which?

By Michaela Muntean

Illustrated by Tom Brannon

Featuring Jim Henson's Sesame Street Muppets

A GOLDEN BOOK • NEW YORK

Published by Golden Books Publishing Company, Inc., in conjunction
with Children's Television Workshop

A portion of the money you pay for this book goes to Children's Television Workshop.
It is put right back into SESAME STREET and other CTW educational projects.
Thanks for helping!

"**L**isten, everybody," said Zoe. "I have a terrific idea for our Halloween costumes."

"Elmo was thinking of being a monster," said Elmo.

"Don't joke me, Elmo," said Zoe. "You *are* a monster."

"Oh, right," said Elmo. "Elmo will have to think of something else."

"Let's all go dressed as witches!" said Zoe.

"It'll be the *trick* part of trick or treat," Zoe explained. "No one will be able to tell who's who because we'll all be dressed the same."

"That will be a good trick!" said Grover. "We will fool everybody."

"Right," said Zoe. "No one will be able to tell *which witch is which!*"

Zoe, Elmo, Telly, Grover, and Herry worked hard on their costumes. They made long black capes and pointy hats. They found frizzy fright wigs, warty noses, and, of course, some brooms.

On Halloween five witches set out to go trick-or-treating.
Their first stop was the lobby of the Furry Arms Hotel.

"Trick!" they said to Sherry Netherland.

"What about the treat?" she asked.

"First comes the trick," said one of the witches. "Guess which witch is Grover."

Sherry pointed to one of the witches. "Is it you?"

"No!" cried the five witches.

"Well, you sure tricked me," said Sherry, and she gave each of them a candied apple.

The elephant elevator operator couldn't guess which witch was Telly.

So he gave each of the witches a bag of peanuts.

Up and down Sesame Street went the five witches. At every stop they tried their trick, but no one could guess which witch was Telly . . .

or Grover . . .

or Zoe . . .

or Elmo . . .

or Herry.

Their trick-or-treat bags were getting heavier and heavier.

"This is the best Halloween ever," said Zoe, and she spun around, swirling her long black cape.

Herry and Telly laughed in a cackling, witchy way.

Elmo and Grover pretended they were riding their brooms.

Their next stop was Oscar's trash can.
"Trick!" they cried.
Oscar peered out from under his trash can lid. "What kind of trick?" he asked suspiciously.

"Guess which witch is Herry," said the five witches.
"That's easy," said Oscar. "Let me see your feet."
Oscar guessed that the witch with the big blue feet
was Herry.

"Grover is the one with the little blue feet," he said. "Bright pink feet? That has to be Telly. The one with little red feet could only be Elmo. That leaves one witch with orange feet, which must belong to Zoe."

"You're right," said the five witches.

"Of course I'm right," said Oscar. "Grouches are grouchy, not stupid. Now I don't have to give you a treat."

"Aw, come on, Oscar," complained the five witches.

"Grumble all you want," said Oscar. "It's music to my ears! Just remember that it's trick *or* treat, not trick *and* treat."

"You're right again," the five witches said sadly, and they began to walk away.

"Okay—wait!" Oscar called after them. "Because
I'm such a bighearted grouch, I've changed my mind."

He disappeared inside his trash can and returned a minute later with a platter of little sandwiches.

"Here's your treat," he said, "but first I have a trick for *you*. Guess which sandwich is which."

"Do you have peanut butter and jelly?" asked the witch with the little red feet. "That is Elmo's favorite."

"No," said Oscar, "but I do have chocolate and
tuna fish, sardine and garlic, and eggplant and prune."
"Yucch!" said the five witches.

"What's the matter?" asked Oscar. "I thought witches would like sand*wiches* for a treat."

"Well," said Zoe, "I guess this time the *trick* is on us!"